Fly High
Butterfly

Balboa Press books may be ordered through booksellers or by contacting:

Balboa Press
A Division of Hay House
1663 Liberty Drive
Bloomington, IN 47403
www.balboapress.com
844-682-1282

ISBN: 978-1-9822-5239-7 (sc)
ISBN: 978-1-9822-5240-3 (e)

Library of Congress Control Number: 2020914354

Print information available on the last page.

Balboa Press rev. date: 08/21/2020

BALBOA.PRESS
A DIVISION OF HAY HOUSE

Fly High
Butterfly

Ricki Renee Brathwaite

Thank you to my family for listening and supporting me. Thank you, Mom, for helping me.

There once was a pretty
butterfly and
her name was Rose; she
lived in a box with plants.

Her favorite color was blue.
It reminded her of her mother.
She is a blue butterfly
that likes to fly.

Her mother use to sing her a song
called "Sweet Love." She would
sing the melody before she goes
to bed.

One day she met a little girl
named Ricki and she played
with her every day because she
missed her Mom so much.
While they were playing, it
was always on her mind
"Where is my Mom?"

Ricki's mom told her that
they were going on a road
trip to their hometown.
Ricki asked if Rose could come too.
Her mom said yes.

When they arrived, Rose the butterfly went to explore.

She saw a butterfly garden
filled with butterflies.
And guess what else she found?

She found her MOM!
She was sooooo Happy!

THE END...

CPSIA information can be obtained
at www.ICGtesting.com
Printed in the USA
LVHW050008141020
668674LV00009B/560